CU00902804

Compendium of Suspense

Ten Short Murder, Mystery and Suspense Stories

GRANT BREMNER

Copyright © 2015 Grant Bremner

All rights reserved. No part of this publication may be reproduced, stored in a retrieval system, or transmitted in any form or by any means, electronic, mechanical, photocopying, recording, or otherwise, without the prior permission of the author.

All characters in this publication are fictitious and any resemblance to real persons, living or dead, is purely coincidental.

ISBN-13: 978-1515265825
ISBN-10: 151526582X

ABOUT THE AUTHOR

Grant Bremner was born in Aberdeen, Scotland, but spent his entire working life with the BBC, mostly in London, in a variety of positions within film and television.

He took early retirement due to a worsening back problem and settled in Spain with his wife Sue where he began to write seriously. After 20 years in the sunshine they returned to the cooler climate of Cheshire. His short stories have won awards and this, together with his other novels and books, can be found at amazon.co.uk.

For more information visit his website:

www.grantbremner.co.uk

ACKNOWLEDGEMENTS

To my wife Sue, as always, for her continued help and support in publishing my stories.

* * *

To Congleton U3A Creative Writing Group for encouraging me to publish these short stories.

Introduction

This compilation of short stories will keep you utterly enthralled and have you turning the pages quickly as you search for the truth within each of them. The stories are uniquely different ranging from ghosts, murders, detectives, luck, and mystery, all structured within everyday life.

The Priest

The priest felt an involuntary shudder pass through his whole body bringing with it the usual sense of guilt and shame that he always experienced when he remembered the last time he had visited Mrs Rutherford some twenty years past. Could it really have been that long since he had last visited this place, this house which left him feeling so cold and terrified that he clasped his bible close to his chest. Now, as he stood looking up at the hideous gargoyles that adorned the façade of Rutherford Manor, he regretted his decision in agreeing to visit the old woman, even if she was dying. This house and its past history was not something he cared to remember. He had only reluctantly agreed to venture out to this house on this dark and dismal night when the pleading tearful voice of Mrs Rutherford's companion sobbing on the telephone had tugged at his conscience.

He stepped forward out of the rain and rang the doorbell, wishing even more strongly now that he had not given an undertaking to attend the old woman, as memories of their one and only meeting began to overwhelm his troubled and tormented mind. He had rejected her plea, she had been toying with him, he had not seen any remorse in her dark eyes. Oh, she had begged enough, even when she had kneeled at his feet beseeching him he had closed his ears to her pleas. He remembered rushing from the house in terror in order to get away from her, afraid of what he might do. Yet, he had always known that there had been another force - an unseen strong presence that had encouraged him to flee the house and to refuse her demand.

Now it was her companion who answered his ring and bid him enter the house. He hesitated as his courage began to falter yet again but the pleading look in the eyes of the companion drew him slowly inside the old house. She took his wet coat, shook it gently before folding it and placing it carefully on a small side table adjacent to the telephone.

She had been crying, her eyes were red and bloated and her face was lined where the tears had worn a path through the heavy make-up that she wore. The priest had not met her on his previous visit all those years ago but if the village gossip was correct, which it usually was, then she had been Mrs Rutherford's constant companion since the night of the accident. He followed her companion slowly along the hall and up the aged oak staircase which creaked and groaned with each step that he took, it did not register in his mind that it was only his steps on the stairs that were making a noise. The portraits on the staircase wall were a mixture of male and female ancestors of the Rutherford line dating back to the middle of the seventeenth century. As he passed by the paintings he had an uncanny feeling that they were studying him in closer detail than he was studying them.

Once more a strong shudder overwhelmed him, but of such force this time that he almost lost his balance and, had it not been for the desperate lunge for the banister with both hands, it would have been he and not his Bible that fell and tumbled slowly to the bottom of the staircase. The priest looked down to where the Bible had fallen and decided to carry on without it as he could not muster the strength and courage he would require to pass by those prying eyes of the generations of Rutherfords again, it would be bad enough when the time came to leave the manor house. So he continued his progress slowly and shakily until he had at last reached the top of the winding staircase, his left hand holding the banister securely.

Mrs Rutherford's companion entered the second door to the left along the darkened landing holding the door ajar to let him enter. The priest bent his head as he entered the dimly lit room thus avoiding the silent pleading eyes of the companion who had noticed that he no longer held his Bible. When he had done so she closed the door behind him and he heard her footsteps receding. The room appeared to be of much the same appearance as when he had first entered it all those years ago. It was dark, illuminated only by two candles, one on each side of the large antique four-poster bed where Mrs Rutherford lay, dying. She was propped up by several bulbous pillows behind her head and neck. Her face was heavy with make-up, although it did not obscure the deep-set wrinkles. Her eyes were closed and her breathing was shallow and laboured. As he walked slowly across the carpeted room he saw her eyes open and she lifted an arm slowly and beckoned him to come closer.

He stopped suddenly as if he had walked into an unseen barrier, his mind in turmoil. An overwhelming multitude of thoughts implored him to turn away from her and leave at once. Was this his guilt for failing to do his duty all those years ago? He decided it was and struggled forward against the unseen force that hindered his progress, until he stood at the bedside looking down at her. He could see that she was frail and weak, her lips were cracked and dried, she was close to death, he had seen death many times. Mrs Rutherford opened her mouth as if to speak but the priest heard only laboured breathing. He bent his head and placed it close to hers and was just able to hear her. He studied her closely, there was no mockery now, her eyes showed nothing but pure undeniable fear. She did not plead nor did she beg as she had done on their first meeting. The priest's emotions, as he knelt down to give her absolution for her sins, were pity and shame. Shame that he had refused her once against his faith and teachings, but who the pity was for, him or her, he did not really know.

There had been arrogance in her tone twenty years ago when she had made her confession to him. It was as if she was boasting that she had got away with the murder of her husband and their two children, in order that she and her lover would reap the rewards of Rutherford Manor. That her lover had deserted her when she had informed him of her evil deed seemed to him to be her only regret. That the police had believed that there had been a terrible accident with the car - a lady such as her did not meddle with brakes - made her arrogant and above the law. Shocked and stunned by the murders and her so-called confession to him, he had, against his faith and teachings, refused her the absolution that she had sought. She had even offered him money, he told her that she would burn in hell for her wicked, sinful act and that he could never forgive her for what she had confessed. He had thought she was lying to him when she had said that she was in constant torment and was haunted by the ghosts of her children and husband, trying to trick him into giving her what she wanted.

He had struggled with his conscious many times over the years about his refusal to grant Mrs Rutherford absolution and had set out for the Manor on numerous occasions to grant her request. But on each occasion, as he approached the long winding drive that led to the manor, some unseen force had always turned him away or just maybe it had been conscience. Tonight he shuddered once more as she made her horrid confession of murder and guilt. It took longer this time as she struggled with her laboured breathing but eventually when it was over he gave her what she wanted and with a heavy heart he granted her absolution from her sins, something for which she had waited for the past twenty years. It would not matter to her that he did not have his Bible in his hands nor his silver cross. Now as he looked down at her wrinkled dead body he felt relieved that at long last he had done his duty for, although the horror of her crimes had tortured him once more, he had seen the fear she carried within replaced by relief in her eyes for a brief moment before death had taken her.

Stepping back from the bed he stumbled on the rug and fell backwards onto the floor. Above him he saw dark mysterious shapes ebbing and flowing, twisting and turning, growing ever stronger until they filled the entire room. Incandescent beings floated over him swaying, swirling ever nearer towards him. He tried vainly to rise but an enormous invisible force kept him pinned firmly to the floor and he began to experience a sharp pain in his chest and found difficulty in breathing. The pressure expanded within the dim room, as did the pain, yet through the pain he heard a child's voice shrieking venomously at him, 'You should not have come back Priest, we tried to warn you to keep away. But the wrong you have done this day will remain with you always, for we shall stay with you forever to remind you of your sin. There shall be no respite, no absolution for you - ever. We shall see to that, priest,' the voice hissed.

The pressure intensified as the demonic visions taunted and tortured him until they slowly relented and the priest lay quaking, wet with fear on the floor, unable to move, his whole body rigid. Blessed unconsciousness took hold of the priest and gave him relief momentarily from his tormentors. He was woken when the door opened and the companion walked slowly and cautiously into the room. He looked at the bed and his memory came flooding back and although exhausted both mentally and physically he managed to get to his feet and fled from that terrifying room, down the stairs leaving his Bible where it had fallen. He flung open the front door and rushed headlong out into the rain and the dark night leaving his coat behind.

Any close observer would have sworn on oath that the faint incandescent outlines of two children and a man hovered directly above the priest as he ran down the long curving drive in abject terror.

The Expert

You show you've got a talent, something you're good at, a job nobody else wants to do and what happens, you get stuck with it. That was the problem he thought as he walked through dark and wet streets to the job he been given. They never let you move on because that would create a vacancy in the organisation with nobody skilful enough to fill it. So you find yourself stuck doing the same job, day in, day out. I certainly hadn't pictured making a career out of it whilst I was still an apprentice as it were, learning the ropes. I'd thought the same as everyone else back then I expect, nice house in the suburbs, nothing too grand, maybe a three bedroomed detached with attached garage plus a nice car, nothing that would attract too much attention, perhaps a Ford Fiesta or a Vauxhall Astra. A wife of course, followed by kids, but who was I kidding, here I was stuck in a rut, a bloke nobody even wanted to think about until they were desperate and had nowhere else to turn.

The rain was easing off as I approached what I thought was the correct house, a three storied semi-detached Victorian in need of repair. The light outside the front door illuminated the number and the bell, this was the address I'd be given earlier. I stood taking in the surroundings before walking up the short path. Several cars were parked in the dimly lit street, tall trees lined the pavement throwing their shadows onto hedges. Satisfied I walked purposefully to the front door and rang the bell. Footsteps, then the door opened with a faint creak.

'You him?' the man behind the door asked.

I nodded and pushed my way past, it didn't pay to linger on the doorstep. 'Yes I'm him,' I replied as I took off my wet coat and hung it on a spare hook on the wall.

He was short, overweight, his belly hung over his trouser belt, he was also nervous. 'I've been waiting for you, I didn't know what to do,' he said as he stood there wringing his chubby hands together.

'Have you touched anything,' I ask before bending down and taking off my shoes.

'Only what I was told to do. You have to hurry, we don't have long, my son might be back any moment,' he said jerkily.

Typical I thought, here we go again, not even the offer of a glass of tap water when I arrive. Normal civility would be expecting too much. Get on with it then, clear off, get out of my house, that was the norm. Sometimes the money was actually thrown at him.

'You alone,' I enquire picking up my bag.

'Yes but my boy will be back soon, he's at the pub with a mate.'

'It's Saturday, I doubt he'll be back before eleven, we have time. You know I don't clear up the mess, you have to.'

His eyes watered over, maybe he was thinking of what he'd done or what he still had to do, I don't know. 'Yes, I understand, I was told that when I rang.'

'Right then you'd better go and get yourself an alibi.'

'Really,' he said surprised, 'what will you be doing?'

I unzip my duffle bag. 'It will take me about an hour. Then I'll lock the house and get into the car your wife drives. You'll read in tomorrow's paper or hear on the radio about the car being found. Soon as you see or hear, you call the police. Where are the keys?'

He fumbled in his trouser pocket then pulled out two sets of keys. 'This is the house,' he handed over a set, 'and these are for the car, it's a Renault.'

'This is for you,' I pull a black garbage bag out of the duffle and hand it to him.

He's reluctant to take it, I can see he's edgy. 'It's for my change of clothes,' I explain.

He doesn't take the bag, he just stands there shifting from foot to foot. He's gone pale.

'Have you changed your mind? It's all the same to me but there will be something to pay.'

'No, no,' he looked aghast at the thought of it.

'Then what's up?'

'I don't really know, maybe I should be doing something.'

'Yes, get out of here. Go somewhere where it's public, a pub, not the one your son is at obviously. Whatever you do don't go near your girlfriend's place, that's taboo, off limits for the time being.' The man's eyes darted towards me, then down again. He was just the same as the rest, another loser. 'Watch a match on the TV in the pub, make people notice you, order the wrong drink, stuff like that, you need people to remember you.' God forbid, here I am in a dead end job explaining things that should come natural to a bloke who should know better, what a life. 'You won't forget my money before you go.'

'It's in the living room.'

I follow him down the short hall into the living room, why do we call it that I wonder? Most folks just sit there watching mindless television all night, that's not living. The room is tastefully decorated I suppose, although not to my liking. It has one of those pictures of an oriental female in a sarong posing on a beach, hanging above a coal effect fire, you see them in all the shops these days, not my taste though. He gets the money from a drawer in the sideboard that's festooned with photos in different frames, family members I suppose. There's no envelope, it's held by a rubber band, he throws the money to me. I flick casually through the large wad of notes.

'It's all there, as agreed on the phone,' he said.

I know it's not necessary to count it, it will all be there, it always is. Nobody would ever think of trying to cheat me, I mean a man in my line of work. 'It was in here, yes?' I ask the question even though I know the answer.

He looks away from me, he doesn't want eye contact. 'Yes, I didn't mean to do it, it was an accident,' he said uncertainly.

Most of them say that, it was never their fault. I guess they have to try and justify it to themselves at least. 'You've done a good job in here, looks normal.'

He hesitates, 'Well I did my best, Bert said to put things back the way they were. It got out of hand you see, the argument...'

I cut him off, I don't want to know any of the sordid details, I never do. It wouldn't be the truth anyway, well not the complete truth. 'We must get on.' I put the wad in a side pocket of my duffle bag. 'You ready?'

He nods nervously and I follow him back into the hallway and up the stairs in my socks. 'Which door?' I ask looking around.

He points, 'That one, Bert said it was best, makes things easier or something,' he replied.

Bert likes to give advice, it's necessary in this game to keep a clear mind. 'Your son, from your first marriage?' I ask as I open the bathroom door.

He looks surprised. 'How did you know?'

'Saw his picture downstairs. Big age gap.' I turn the bathroom light on and walk in. She was in the bath, her left leg dangling over the side of the bath, toe nails painted pink. The eyes were wide open, staring, the bruises on her neck clearly visibly. I put my bag on the floor.

'Hold it,' he said from behind my shoulder, 'she's still got her ring.'

I look at the left hand and see a silver band with diamonds, expensive I thought. 'You have to leave it on,' I said raising my voice slightly.

'It was very expensive,' he blurts out, his face reddening, 'do we have to?'

I turn around and look at him. 'I want you to understand what I'm saying. You can't give the ring to your girlfriend, neither can you sell it. Just forget about the damned ring.' Miserable cheapskate I thought. There were times when I felt sorry for some of them, others I would have liked to make disappear permanently. He stood there, wringing his hands again looking down at the tiled floor. I open my bag and take out the saw. I'll pocket the ring when he's gone, call it a bonus.

'I can't believe this is happening,' he said softly just before he began to cry.

'Pull yourself together,' I say harshly as I put down the saw, 'you have to go out to a pub and act like you don't have a care in the world. Come on you can do it,' I say encouragingly resisting the temptation to put a hand on his shoulder.

He nodded then wiped his nose on his shirtsleeve before taking a deep breath, 'Thanks for your help, Bert said you were the best.'

'I am,' I said. That was why I'd gotten into this rut. Just go out there and try and find someone else like me who has the skill to take a body apart like a butcher with a lamb, hide the bits so that police dogs couldn't sniff them out and to cap it all, play father confessor to the guilty. I picked up my saw. 'You must go, you certainly won't want to see the rest of this.'

Invitation to Dinner

The snow started just as Gary drove his Mercedes into the drive of a large Victorian mansion house. A slight tremble went through Gary's body as he parked the car, a glance at his watch informed him that he was already twenty minutes late. He briefly wondered what they might think of him for being tardy, but then dismissed it, he would make a plausible excuse, he was good at that.

'Sorry to keep you waiting, Gary, and in the snow, I was in the kitchen turning the oven down. Do come in. My, you are wet my dear,' remarked Olivia as she opened the front door.

'Sorry to be late, the traffic was bad due to the snow,' he lied easily, wondering if she'd deliberately kept him standing out in the now heavier falling snow.

'Why don't you go and dry off, you know where the facilities are,' suggested Olivia lightly.

'Good idea,' said Gary as he headed for the downstairs bathroom.

'He's drying off, he'll be here in a moment,' said Olivia as she walked into the dining room.

'How does he appear?' enquired Granville gruffly.

'A little uneasy I would say, shall you pour him a drink?'

'Of course my dear, whisky and soda I believe,' said Granville as he turned to the drinks trolley. 'Your usual Olivia?'

'Thanks Granville, I'll just see to the roast, be nice when he appears.' Olivia looked Granville directly in his eyes before leaving for the kitchen.

'Ah, there you are my boy, here I've poured you a drink,' said Granville in a friendly tone as Gary entered the dining room.

'Thanks, I could with one,' he said as he took hold of the glass. 'Your Christmas decorations look wonderful. Cheers!'

'Oh really! Well, good health my boy,' said Granville, although good health was the last thing he wished for Gary.

'How's business?' Granville's tone had changed, it sounded harsh.

Gary noted the change and wasn't surprised. It was, after all, Granville's money that had kept the business running. 'We are doing rather well, signed a new contract only last week worth two million, so I can't complain,' answered Gary lightly. Whatever happened this evening he was not going to fall out with Granville.

'Pleased to hear it my boy, although it's a great pity that Susan is not here to share in your success,' said Granville staring intently at Gary.

Gary looked at Granville wondering if he had made the right decision in coming here this evening. He could so easily have made an excuse when the snow had started. Susan had died eight months ago and Gary was aware that her parents blamed him for the accident, especially as the money in her trust fund transferred to her new husband instead of reverting back to her father. However, there had been a thorough investigation by the police and no blame had been attached to him.

'I'm truly sorry that she is not here to share in the success also, I miss her you know,' said Gary with a degree of honesty. He missed Susan because she had been great at getting new clients for the business, he had just been lucky.

'Do you Gary? I heard that you have a new girlfriend, already,' remarked Olivia caustically as she appeared from the kitchen with a bowl of salad.

He was surprised that they knew about Glenda, he'd thought that he had managed to keep her well hidden.

'Of course I miss her, Olivia,' he tried to sound convincing. 'She was the world to me, but life must go on and I've only had a couple of dates. My psychiatrist suggested it might help me forget the past.'

'Really, he suggested Glenda! Well I guess that's modern living for you,' said Olivia sarcastically.

'No of course he didn't suggest Glenda. He said I needed to get out more, see other people, that kind of thing,' retorted Gary.

'It's not even a year Gary and,' Olivia paused for dramatic effect, 'oh dear, do forgive me, we invited you for dinner as a friend and here we are about to argue. Please sit down and I'll bring in the roast, it's your favourite, lamb.'

'Thanks,' said Gary as he watched Olivia head off for the kitchen.

'Sorry about that Gary but you have to understand that we loved Susan very much. Of course you must get on with your life, sit down my boy,' said Granville cordially.

Gary finished his drink in one go and sat down in the chair that Granville had indicated. He was going to remain calm no matter what they said to him. He wasn't going to let them get the better of him. 'How are things with you Granville? Are you enjoying your retirement? Playing golf now?'

'No to the golf and no, I am not enjoying my retirement, so things are not going so well really,' replied Granville heavily.

'Sorry to interrupt you my dear but could you do the honours?' enquired Olivia as she approached the table with the roast lamb displayed on a silver platter.

'Of course my dear,' said Granville as he picked up the carving knife.

Gary was grateful that during dinner there was no more mention of Susan or his new girlfriend Glenda. Granville had even opened up a couple of bottles of Château Le Gay 1990, a wine that Gary usually ordered when he was out to impress potential clients. In fact the evening had turned out much better than Gary had thought it would. All he had to do now was have a coffee then be on his way.

'You'll have a coffee Gary before you go?' enquired Olivia politely.

'That would be very nice, thank you,' replied Gary languidly as the alcohol he'd consumed had already begun to take effect. 'That was a very pleasant meal Olivia, the lamb was just perfect.'

'I'm so pleased that you liked it,' said Olivia as she paused by the door. 'Granville be a dear and get Gary a nice brandy to go with his coffee.'

'I'm not sure I should Granville,... what with the wine,... I am driving,' stated Gary hesitantly.

'Just a small one then, it's only a Calvados,' said Granville as he stood up and walked towards the drinks trolley where he poured a large measure into a brandy glass.

'Can I use your bathroom?' Gary asked as he stood up from the table.

'Be my guest.' Granville watched Gary walk unevenly into the hall then took a small phial from his breast pocket, opened it and poured its contents into the brandy glass.

'Here we are,' said Olivia as she walked back into the dining room. 'Is everything all right?' she enquired when she noticed that Gary was not present.

Granville beamed her a smile and held up the empty phial. 'Gary is in the toilet dear, everything is fine.'

Gary was feeling quite smug, the evening had gone much better than he'd expected. He was aware that his ex in-laws didn't care for him much, they had made that clear at the reading of Susan's will. It had come as a shock to them that Susan had made a will leaving Gary all of the money in her trust fund set up by her father. The lawyer had explained that it was perfectly legal, although he had assumed that Susan had spoken to her father about it. Gary walked back into the dining room and took his seat. 'Most hospitable Granville, cheers,' he said before taking a hefty swig from the brandy glass.

'Down the hatch dear boy,' said Granville cheerfully as he took an envelope from his jacket pocket. 'I have something here that might interest you Gary.'

'I don't think I have time for that Granville, I have an early meeting tomorrow, I had better go,' he started to rise but somehow found he couldn't move a muscle.

Granville beamed down at him, 'Oh I think you can spare us some more of your valuable time Gary. You have only a few seconds before all of your muscles seize up, anything you want to say?'

Gary began to panic, this couldn't be happening, they'd been so nice during dinner, was this a joke?

'What have you done to...,' was all he managed to say before complete paralysis took hold.

Olivia walked over to where Granville was standing and looked down at Gary. She could see the fear in his eyes, the man was terrified out of his wits. 'Well done Granville,' she said cheerfully.

'Yes, it certainly worked and as quickly as I'd hoped. Want to know what I've given you Gary? Of course you do. Well it's something I've been working on these past few months, something to keep me busy in my retirement. It's a derivative of curare, a neuromuscular blocking drug, paralyses the muscles almost instantly, no taste and, best of all, it metabolises quickly leaving no trace in the blood, urine or tissue.' Granville leaned forwards and stared into Gary's terrified eyes.

Gary couldn't believe what he was hearing, this can't be happening to me. They were nice people, he'd liked them, he'd liked their money more but hey, what they were doing was wrong. Wait, maybe they were having a joke, yes a joke, surely.'

'It's no joke Gary, just in case you were wondering, we are deadly serious,' Olivia said as she began clearing away the dinner dishes.

'This, my boy, is a report from a private detective,' Granville took a letter from the envelope he'd been holding. 'It makes for very interesting reading. First, he's absolutely certain that you murdered our daughter. He believes he has enough evidence to turn over to the police to guarantee a conviction. But that's not what we want, so you won't be rotting in a gaol for years.' Granville paused and looked into Gary's eyes. 'He found the bottle of Rohypnol you thought you'd destroyed, even had your DNA on it, careless of you really Gary. The skip you threw it in just outside your flat had a computerised chip, apparently the council keeps a check on their movements,' said Olivia as she sat down in her chair directly across from Gary.

This can't be happening, what has that son of a bitch done to me? Jesus, I can't move a bloody thing, hell's teeth they're going to kill me. Why the hell can't I move? Rohypnol doesn't do that, damn it must have been in the brandy and I scoffed the lot. Please god, this can't be happening, thought Gary as he sat unable to move a single muscle.

'Look Olivia he's sweating, it's dripping down his face, pity he can't feel it, the murderer.' Granville glanced at the letter, 'You told us that Susan was going to see a friend by herself, that's why you weren't in the car with her, even said it to the police. But that wasn't true, you were with her in the car. Someone saw you that night. It's taken some time only because they've been out of the country. They stopped you for directions remember? Aha, I see that you do.'

God the detective must have found them. He'd been worried for weeks that they might show up but they hadn't and the police concluded their investigation, accident caused by alcohol, Susan had drunk too much, the coroner had said.

'They said that Susan appeared to be asleep when they spoke to you, but we know that she'd been drugged by you. You put her in the driver's seat, put the car in drive, then watched as it went over the cliff, you heartless bastard,' screamed Granville unable to control his emotions.

Gary knew now that he was a dead man, they had not gone to all this trouble just to scare him and they'd said they weren't going to the police. He remembered that he'd felt no emotion when he'd put the tablets into Susan's drink. He had treated her death as an exercise, trying to get every part of it correct. The couple wanting directions had been traumatic, Susan might have woken up. Moving her into the driver's seat was harder than he'd imagined it would be, but then he'd been lucky as no one else approached the cliff top that evening. Please, I'm sorry, I'm really sorry, I'll let you have her money back, his eyes pleaded silently.

'I'll just take these out to the kitchen dear,' said Olivia evenly as she headed for the door.

'Right, I'll finish up in here.' Granville had regained control of his emotions. 'Now Gary, I want you to know how this will end.' He paused for a moment, his thoughts had drifted to Susan and her untimely and unwarranted death. 'It will be similar to Susan's in some respects, you will die in a car accident, but you are going to commit suicide Gary.' Granville walked around the table and put his hand into Gary's jacket pocket and withdrew his iPhone. 'Very handy these devices, what with e-mail and the like. You are going to send us one just before you drive your car into the lake, which according to the forecast might even freeze tonight. It's easier just now if I do it for you, don't you think? Oh, how remiss of me, of course you can't respond. Let's continue, you are going to say that you can't go on without Susan, Glenda was just a distraction. You felt guilty about cheating on her memory. You put on a brave face, didn't want anyone to know how much you missed her but you can't carry on without her. Olivia and I will confirm that you were very depressed, drank far too much alcohol, we even tried to get you a taxi which you adamantly refused.' Granville sat down next to Gary and opened his iPhone. 'No password, how remiss of you Gary!'

Hell's teeth, why hadn't he put a password on his iPhone, he'd meant to but then he was never that good at remembering passwords, Susan had been the one at work who dealt with them, so Gary could only watch as Granville typed out his suicide letter on his damned iPhone.

'How's it coming dear?' Olivia asked as she pushed a wheelchair into the dining room.

Gary saw the wheelchair from the corner of his eye and tears silently rolled down his cheeks.

'Finished, we'll take him around the back, I'll get his car, we'll dump him in it then I'll drive to the lake. I'll walk back via the golf course, it's only two miles,' said Granville.

'Wear something warm, it's freezing out and drive carefully, the road may be icy in parts and don't forget to wipe the car and the iPhone thoroughly,' said Olivia as she got hold of Gary's right arm.

'No, of course not, and don't you forget about the taxi,' said Granville as he took hold of the left arm.

'I won't, I'll tell them he's changed his mind and is insisting on driving himself, Merry Christmas dear.'

Gary began to scream as loud as he could, yet nobody heard him.

A Game of Chance

It's a hot and humid day and I really and truthfully hate my wife.

We're playing Scrabble. That's how bad it is. I'm forty-two years old, it's a blistering hot and humid Sunday afternoon and all I can think of to do with my life is to play Scrabble with my lousy wife. I should be out, doing exercise, spending money, meeting people. I don't think I've spoken to anyone except my wife since Thursday morning. On Thursday morning I spoke to the milkman.

My letters are crap. I play, appropriately, BEGIN. With the N on the little pink star. Twenty-two points.

I watch my wife's smug expression as she rearranges her letters. Clack, clack, clack. I hate her. If she wasn't around, I'd be doing something interesting right now. I'd be climbing Mount Kilimanjaro. I'd be starring in the latest Hollywood blockbuster. I'd be sailing the Vendée Globe on a sixty foot clipper called the New Horizons - I don't know, but I'd be doing something exciting, interesting, not staring down at a Scrabble board.

She plays JINXED, with the J on a double-letter and scores 30 points. She's beating me already. Maybe I should kill her.

If only I had a D, then I could play MURDER. That would be a sign. That would be permission. I start chewing on my U. It's a bad habit I know. All the letters are frayed but I can't stop myself. I play WARMER for 22 points, mainly so I can keep chewing on my U. As I'm picking new letters from the bag, I find myself thinking the letters will tell me what to do. If they spell out KILL, or STAB, or her name, or anything, I'll do it right now. I'll finish her off and to hell with the consequences.

My rack spells MIHZPA. Plus the U in my mouth. Damn no use at all.

The heat of the sun is pushing at me through the window. I can hear buzzing insects outside. I hope they're not bees. My cousin Harold swallowed a bee when he was nine, his throat swelled up and he died. I hope that if they are bees, they fly into my wife's throat.

She plays SWEATIER, using all her letters. 24 points plus a 50 point bonus sod it. If it wasn't too hot to move I would strangle her right now. I am getting sweatier. It needs to rain, to clear the air. As soon as that thought crosses my mind, I find a good word, HUMID on a double-word score, using the D of JINXED. The U makes a little splash of saliva when I put it down. Another 22 points for me. I really hope she has lousy letters.

She opens her mouth and tells me she has lousy letters. For some reason I can't explain, I hate her more.

Now she plays FAN, with the F on a double-letter and gets up to fill the kettle and turn on the air-conditioning. It's the hottest day for ten years and my wife is turning on the kettle. This is why I hate my wife. I play ZAPS, with the Z doubled and she gets a static shock off the air-conditioning unit, I hear her swear softly. I find this remarkably satisfying as I somehow manage to restrain myself from laughing out loud.

She sits back down with a heavy sigh and starts fiddling with her letters again. Clack clack. Clack clack. I feel a terrible rage build up inside me. Some inner poison slowly spreading through my limbs and when it gets to my fingertips I am going to jump out of my chair spilling the Scrabble tiles over the floor, and I am going to start hitting her again and again and again with the board.

The rage gets to my fingertips and passes. My heart is beating faster. I'm sweating. I think my face actually twitches. Then I sigh, deeply, and sit back into my chair. The kettle starts whistling. As the whistle builds it makes me feel hotter.

Leaning forwards with a smirk on her face she plays READY on a double-word for 18 points, then goes to pour herself a cup of tea. No I do not want one I tell her.

I steal a blank tile from the letter bag when she's not looking, and throw back a V from my rack. She gives me a suspicious look. She sits back down with her cup of tea, making a cup-ring on the table, as I play an 8-letter word: CHEATING, using the A of READY. 64 points, including the 50 point bonus, which means I'm beating her now.

She asks me if I cheated, damned cheek. I really, really hate her.

She plays IGNORE on the triple-word for 21 points. The score is 153 to her, 155 to me. The steam rising from her cup of tea makes me feel hotter. I try to make murderous words with the letters on my rack, but the best I can do is SLEEP.

My wife sleeps all the time. She slept through an argument our next-door neighbours had that resulted in a broken door, a smashed TV and a Teletubby Lala doll with all the stuffing coming out. And then she bitched at me for being moody the next day from lack of sleep.

If only there was some way for me to get rid of her. I increased the insurance policy last year, tripled it.

I spot a chance to use all my letters. EXPLODES, using the X of JINXED. 72 points. That'll show her.

As I put the last letter down, there is a deafening bang and the air-conditioning unit fails.

My heart is racing, but not from the shock of the bang. I don't believe it - but it can't be a coincidence. The letters made it happen. I played the word EXPLODES and it happened, the air-conditioning unit actually exploded. And before, I played the word CHEATING when I cheated. And then ZAP when my wife got the electric shock. The words are coming true, they are definitely coming true. The letters are choosing their future. The whole game is JINXED.

My wife plays SIGN, with the N on a triple-letter, for 10 points.

I have to test this. I have to play something and see if it happens again. Something unlikely, to prove that the letters are making it happen. My rack is ABQYFWE. That doesn't leave me with a lot of options. I start frantically chewing on the B.

I play FLY, using the L of EXPLODES. I sit back in my chair and close my eyes, waiting for the sensation of rising up from my chair. Waiting to fly.

Stupid. I open my eyes, and there's a fly. An insect, buzzing around above the Scrabble board, surfing the weak thermals from the now tepid cup of tea. That proves nothing. The fly could have been there anyway.

I need to play something unambiguous. Something that cannot be misinterpreted. Something absolute and final. Something terminal. Something murderous.

My wife plays CAUTION, using a blank tile for the N. 18 points.

The letters on my rack are AQWEUK, plus the B in my mouth. I am awed by the power of the letters, and frustrated that I cannot wield it. Maybe I should cheat again, and pick out the letters I need to spell SLASH or SLAY.

Then suddenly out of the blue it hits me. The perfect word. A powerful, dangerous, terrible word. I play QUAKE for 19 points.

I wonder if the strength of the quake will be proportionate to how many points it scored. I can feel the trembling energy of potential in my veins. I am commanding fate. I am manipulating destiny I feel myself shaking, trembling with excitement.

My wife plays DEATH for 34 points, just as the room starts to shake before my eyes. I gasp with surprise and vindication and the B that I was chewing on gets lodged firmly in my throat. I try to cough. My face goes red, then blue. My throat swells. I draw blood clawing at my neck. The earthquake builds to a climax. I'm shaking all over then I fall to the floor.

My wife smiles as she sits there watching me.

I'm lying on the floor gasping for breath looking desperately up at my wife. My wife just sits there, watching and waiting for me to take my last breath, the bitch.

Fête

She'd already made up her mind they were going to drop by the church Fête no matter her daughter's remonstrations.

'Don't be ridiculous Carol, just because you interviewed him doesn't mean we can't go. He's such a wonderful man Carol, does an awful lot for local charities so I'm told.' Mrs Foster quickened her step, 'They have a tombola you know, I won two prizes last year.'

Carol's mind flashed back to the interview when she'd accompanied Chief Inspector Jennings to the rectory two weeks ago to the day. It had been lashing down and by the time they'd got from the car to the front door they were both soaking wet. The reverend had taken their wet coats and placed them on an indoor clothes line above the Aga in the large well-apportioned kitchen. 'I expect you've come to see me about James,' he'd said calmly before insisting we had a cup of tea first.

The interview hadn't lasted long and I was more of an observer than anything else. Jennings had started by saying a complaint had been received from one of the choir boy's mother that her son had come home later than usual from practice, dishevelled and slightly distressed and had gone straight to his room. She'd questioned him at length and eventually he'd told her that he thought he'd been interfered with. Reverend Lovejoy had laughed it off, explaining the boys had been playing a ball game in the vestry after practice and he'd roundly told them off and sent them home.

'Why did you know it was the boy James we wanted to talk to you about?' Jennings had asked with notebook in hand.

'Well his mother came to see me and made some serious accusations. So after I'd explained about the ball game I told her if she wasn't satisfied to see you, well the police,' he'd replied before taking a sip of tea. I only noticed his hand was shaking because the teacup rattled gently on the saucer as he held it. Plus he never looked the Chief Inspector directly in the eye.

'Good advice Reverend, never get involved with parents making wicked accusations, leave it to us professionals.' The Chief Inspector finished his tea. 'Have you ever been alone with the boy Reverend?'

'Alone! No, I don't think so,' he hesitated a few moments after raising his eyebrows, 'well, perhaps he might have been the last to leave on the odd occasion, a few seconds behind the others,' he shrugged his broad shoulders.

'Of course, well that's the nature of things isn't it? You understand reverend we have to check out any allegations of sexual impropriety. Come on Constable Foster we've a few more to interview,' the Chief Inspector took his and her coat from the dryer. 'Thank you reverend you've been most hospitable. I'm sure we'll get to the bottom of this, no need to show us out we can find our own way.'

A brief look of relief spread across the reverend's face like butter on hot toast, then it was gone, but Carol had seen how relieved he'd been for that fleeting moment when she'd been putting on her coat that was by now very nearly dry.

On the way out they passed through the main hallway and Carol noticed a laptop computer sitting on a table in the dining room, pictures were constantly changing like they do in a photo slide show. 'Excuse me, I've a sermon to finish,' said the reverend as he pushed roughly past her and closed the lid of the laptop.

'He looked nervy sir and did you see how quickly he shut the lid of his computer, pushed past me like he'd suddenly remembered it,' I said to the Chief Inspector as we walked back to the car, luckily the rain had stopped.

'A policeman asks you questions about possible sexual irregularities and even you'd get nervous Foster and you didn't see any naked boys on the laptop, did you?'

'No sir, landscapes but he looked shifty to me.'

'Well praise the lord, looking shifty isn't yet evidence in a court of law. The background check we did on him is clean, model citizen by all accounts. We've got other parents to interview, who's next on the list.'

Now she and her mother were about to shake his hand as Reverend Lovejoy stood by the entrance to the church grounds. 'Come on Carol stop lagging behind we'll have our coffee after.'

'So pleased you've come to support the Fête,' intoned the Revered in a smooth and silky voice to my mum as he handed over the regulatory raffle ticket in exchange for the two pound coin proffered.

'Ah, it's er..., PC Fisher, isn't it, we met the other week,' he said to me hesitantly as I paid my money.

'Foster, and yes sir, it was me.' I avoided direct eye contact.

'I guess that business is finished then,' he said quietly looking around him.

'I don't know Reverend, it's the Chief Inspector you'd need to talk to. Excuse me, my mum's run off.' I cut short the conversation and hurried up the winding path to where the tents and marquees were set up. Mum was already at the tombola stall.

The investigation was far from concluded, two of the other boys had spoken of other wrongdoings when questioned and more detailed background checks were ongoing. Carol had even suggested the Chief Inspector get a warrant to impound the laptop she'd seen but had been forcibly told there was insufficient evidence to support such a request. Since then she'd been re-assigned to traffic due to the flu causing a shortage of staff in that department.

'Carol stop looking at the house and come and help me open these tickets, I don't know why they have to put so much sellotape around them, takes an age to open them,' shouted mum as I took in the scene around me. There were probably around one hundred or so people present, a lot of kids with their mums although there were some reluctant fathers also, mooching about with hands in pockets. How ironic I thought, I'm definitely not a kid no matter what mum thinks. Struggling with the tape I noticed the kitchen door to the manse was ajar as two women in white aprons flitted in and out with trays carrying cupcakes and the like.

'Oh Carol look, number sixty-five, that's a winner. Have you got any ending with a five?'

Without looking I handed her back the pile she'd given me. 'No mum, you have a go at these, I need the toilet, I'll be back in a moment.' I didn't give her a chance to argue as I quickly walked towards the kitchen door passing the portable toilets as I went.

'The icing on this cupcake is delicious Mavis you must let me have your recipe, mine always comes out soggy, if you know what I mean? The sound of the women talking disappeared as they reached the first tent where the coconut shy was located. By then I was through the kitchen and heading for the dining room where I'd last seen the laptop, it wasn't there. The next room was obviously the reverend's study as it contained a desk, leather chair, printer and the laptop was closed, much to my dismay. I opened the lid then switched it on, knowing there was bound to be a password. There was, blinking away in front of me, what on earth could it be? I looked around the room for inspiration but there was nothing there save old furniture and books. Then I had an idea, Lovejoy. So with trembling fingers I typed in antiques and hit the return button. I was impressed I'd guessed correctly, the welcome screen appeared. Taking a usb drive from my handbag I inserted it into a vacant slot and hit copy. Damn and blast it, it was going to take twenty-two minutes. From the study window I could see the entrance to the Fête and the reverend was no longer standing there welcoming the arrivals. So with eighteen minutes to go I legged it back through the kitchen picking up a plate of scones on my way out. Whatever else I did I had to ensure Lovejoy didn't discover I was copying his hard drive, my career was dead and buried if he did. I heaved a thankful sigh of relief, he was chatting to a group of elderly women next to the fortune-teller tent.

A heavy hand landed on my shoulder. 'You were a long time Carol, look I've won a box of biscuits and a bottle of wine,' said her excited mother showing off her gains.

'I'd check the sell by date on the biscuits if I were you and use the wine for cooking. Look mum, I want you to do something for me without asking questions, can you do that?' Carol knew she was taking a risk but she needed some insurance.

'Of course dear you only have to ask,' said her mum putting her spoils into a foldable shopping bag she always carried in her handbag.

'Muscle your way into that group,' I pointed to where the women were conversing with the reverend, 'I want you to engage the reverend in conversation and keep him talking until I get back. Can you do that?' Once my mum got started anyone else was lucky to get a single word in.

A look of puzzlement crossed her face slowly before she replied, 'Are you off to the toilet again? Carol are you pregnant? Is that why you want me to keep him talking so you can check if you need to book him,' the questions flowed.

'Mother, don't be silly, just do as I ask, keep him talking.' Carol walked away and offered a scone to a young couple passing. The kitchen thankfully was empty as was the study on her return. The screen showed seven minutes remaining, so I opened up his library and went to pictures where usually everyone who owns a computer stores their photos, it was empty, not even a folder which in itself was very odd. Five minutes left so I entered *.*.jpg into the search box and hit the key. I stood back as I watched hundreds of small icons indicating photographs appear inside the search box. When it finished the search I noticed there were two thousand seven hundred and twenty-two photos. I didn't dare click on one to view as I would be leaving a trace if the reverend checked his laptop. Beep, the tiny sound indicated the copy was done so I grabbed my small drive, shut down the laptop and hurried back to mum in the hope she'd still be talking to the reverend.

'Ah there you are my dear I was just telling Revered Lovejoy here that you are an ace constable, won't be long before you get promoted and that...'

I cut her off, 'Yes mum but I'm sure the reverend has more to do today than chat to you for hours on end.' I spoke cheekily giving a chortle at the end. I was now desperate to get home and check out the drive I had transferred into my handbag.

'There he is, he's the man that abused my little boy,' shouted a distraught woman as she approached the trio. 'I've reported him to the police and they've done nothing, but I know he did it, the pervert.' She took a kitchen knife from her shopping bag and waved it about frantically.

Carol's academy training immediately kicked in. Dropping her bag she disarmed the woman who unsurprisingly did not put up any resistance. Then taking her mobile from her bag she called the station for assistance.

A young male reporter from the local newspaper who'd been covering the Fête ran up with notebook in hand. By the look on his face it was clear he hadn't expected to be covering a knife attack and a sexual accusation. 'Any truth to the accusation you sexually molested her son reverend?' he asked gleefully. He'd been covering events like these for years and had never been gifted a story such as this.

Reverend Lovejoy was clearly shocked by the direct question. 'Ahem, no, er..., no comment,' he managed before turning and running towards his house with a look of desperation on his face.

Events followed swiftly after that, Carol kept the eager reporter at bay when he then tried to question the woman who'd made the allegation. The squad car arrived and took the distraught woman who was now sobbing quietly to the station where she was questioned then released on police bail after her boy had been interviewed separately by specialists. A warrant was issued enabling the Chief Inspector to search the reverend's house and the laptop was impounded. After lunch Carol received a call to go to the station immediately.

'I don't know how long I'll be mum, so don't keep any dinner for me,' said Carol as she put on her overcoat.

'The hard drive's clean PC Foster, he must have deleted the photos after the journalist spoke to him. The young lad's confused and hasn't actually said he was assaulted and there's nothing there we can hold him on,' stated the Chief Inspector pointing to the laptop.

Carol opened her bag and produced the copy of the hard drive, 'Perhaps this might help sir.'

Reverend Lovejoy broke down half an hour later when shown a few of the photographs from the copy of the hard drive Carol had procured from his house. He assumed that police computer experts had managed to recover his files after he'd deleted them.

When Carol returned home later that night with a sound telling-off from the Chief Inspector regarding the manner in which she'd retrieved the evidence still ringing in her ears, she found her mother had ignored her advice about not waiting for dinner. The table was laid, a rich aroma of stewed beef was coming from the slow cooker and a recently opened bottle of red wine was breathing in the warm kitchen. A quick check ensured it was not the wine mum had won at the fête.

'You've had a rough day love, I thought you'd appreciate a nice hot meal when you got home, now sit down and tell me everything that happened at the station.'

Bad Luck

A sharp crack of thunder stirred Nathan from his short restless nap. The incessant hum of tyres on tarmac reminded him of a wasp's nest he'd come across as a boy playing in his Uncle's peach grove. He knew enough to leave the swarming hive alone. Still, the angry insects attacked, leaving him badly stung. Even at that young age, Nathan's inherent bad luck was evident.

The lumbering Greyhound bus lurched from side to side as it rolled down the well-travelled highway. Its rhythmic sway lulled many of the passengers into a comfortable sleep, but not Nathan. 'Bad Luck,' he repeated to himself, 'Bad Luck!'

Born into a poor southern family, Nathan's life was one struggle after another. "The family luck," his father bemoaned often, sitting in his old rocker on the back porch of the small wood-frame home. "If it weren't for bad luck, this family would have no luck."

His father's words stuck with him, as had his luck. For twenty-five years Nathan fought and scratched for everything. But Nathan was a proud man. He never let it get to him. When life knocked him down he recalled his father's words. Then Nathan would stubbornly pick himself up with a renewed sense of determination.

Nathan's bad luck culminated in his being arrested for a crime he didn't commit. He was in the wrong place at the wrong time. A botched investigation, an overworked public defender and an indifferent jury conspired to seal his fate. As the verdict was read, Nathan could hear his father's voice calling from the grave. 'No good deed goes unpunished my boy.'

That was three years ago. Now he was heading home. Nathan pulled the faded, wrinkled photo from his denim shirt pocket. Running his fingers lovingly over the image he smiled. His wife Becky was the only good luck to ever come his way. She was his love; his strength; his life. Even after the arrest and trial, Becky staunchly stood by her husband. She knew he was innocent. That was all that mattered to Nathan. It had seen him through the last three years.

Becky wrote Nathan daily and they spoke on the phone often, but he made her promise not to try and visit him in prison. He didn't want her to see him and think of him this way.

'Everything will be alright when I get home,' he'd calmly assured her. They both knew their love was strong enough to stand the separation.

When it came time for his release Becky pleaded with Nathan to let her be there. Nathan refused. He needed time to himself; time to get used to being free; time to get his head together; time to forget. Though he burned to hold his wife in his arms, the solitude of the long bus ride was what he needed. Nathan's luck held true. The departure was delayed several hours due to a burnt out alternator. A sudden thunderstorm put the late running bus further behind schedule. It was already dark and he still had a long way to go. It was well after midnight when the Greyhound finally pulled up to the all-night diner which served as the small town's bus depot. The sweet fragrance of magnolia greeted Nathan as he alighted from the coach and stepped out into the fresh Carolina air. He breathed deeply taking in lungfuls. The scent reminded him of Becky, and told him he was indeed home at last.

Retrieving his single canvas bag, Nathan headed down the tree-lined country lane that would lead him home. The road was dark and deserted but Nathan knew the way by heart. As he walked he pictured his beautiful wife. She was probably asleep, curled up on the sofa, surrendered to the fatigue of anticipation. It gave Nathan a warm feeling inside. He was already beginning to forget the pain and degradation of the past thirty-six months, putting it out of his mind, ripping out the pages of that chapter of his unlucky life. He was home now.

'Everything will be alright my dear,' he said aloud. His words echoed eerily among the tall pine trees, as if a ghost mocking his very thoughts. Nathan tried his best to shake the uncomfortable feeling.

Half an hour later he turned into the familiar long dirt driveway. The house lay dark, still. As he approached, he noticed the front door stood wide open. Perhaps Becky had been looking out for him. Stepping inside, a faint muffled sound reached Nathan's ears. It came from the back of the house. He could see a light reflected on a wall. Dropping his bag, he hurried down the short hallway. At the master bedroom Nathan felt his heart stop.

An intruder was bent over the cowering figure of his helpless wife. Becky was cruelly tied to the bed. A wide strip of duct tape silenced her terrified screams. Brandishing a large hunting knife, and savagely ripping Becky's nightgown, the attacker wasn't aware of her husband's arrival. Nathan tore across the bedroom. Screaming, he threw himself headlong at the surprised assailant. The lethal knife dropped harmlessly to the floor.

Nathan fought like a madman. Even after the would-be rapist stopped moving, he continued to beat and kick the fiend mercilessly. Nathan probably would have killed the man. Just then Becky's picture slipped from his pocket. It landed on the floor in front of him, bringing Nathan to his senses.

Staggering to his feet, Nathan rushed to his wife's side. 'It's OK baby, it's OK,' he whispered lovingly, softly stroking her flaxen hair. Gently he pulled the tape from her lips and kissed her. He tasted her salty tears, felt her pounding heart and trembling body.

'It's OK... I'm here now. It's over,' he reassured her as he looked down into her eyes. 'Everything's going to be okay.'

Looking around, Nathan spied the hunting knife. Scooping it up, he leaned over the bed and began to cut the ropes binding Becky's hands and feet. Then he heard a noise.

Thinking it was the intruder coming to, Nathan turned. The knife's chrome blade flashed menacingly in his hand. Two uniformed policemen stood in the bedroom doorway, guns drawn.

Becky's scream was obscured by the deafening roar of pistol fire.

The hunting knife slipped from Nathan's fingers. He felt himself punched backwards across the room.

Becky's eyes met Nathan's. He slumped to the floor, blood trickling from his lips.

Bad Luck, no dammed luck ever,' Becky heard her husband say faintly with his last dying breath.

FOREVER YOUNG

He was not a thief. He was not a murderer. Had she not made him a solemn vow, she had promised him he could have the secret - for it was hers and hers alone to give. Yet it was she who had gone back on her word, not him. He had done precisely everything that she had demanded of him, degrading things he thought, yet she was never fully satisfied. There were always other little things that she made him do, that she had told him were essential if he was to possess the secret. He had believed every word that she had spoken, she had chosen him, and him alone, from all the others. For she was, after all, the keeper of the secret.

All who lived in the small village had been afraid of her, but not he - and he never really understood why he alone had no fear of her. His father was a tall, muscular man with broad shoulders and great strength but he walked in fear of her. His loving and devoted mother was clearly terrified of her, the fear that was in his mother's eyes every time they had cause to go near her cottage told him that. Both had told him that she was evil personified and that he must stay away from her in order to protect his soul. He was their only son and they only wanted to protect him from the wicked woman that lived in the small dark cottage on the edge of the forest.

The teacher at school had continually warned all the children about the danger of straying too near to the dark cottage, which was always shrouded in shadow by the tall trees. She is evil the teacher told the class, never ever go to her, if she calls out do not tarry to hear what she might say. Ignore her pleas for companionship in her wanderings through the forest and the fields. For she is an evildoer who will prey on the fertile minds of young children for her condemnable lustful wicked ways. This the teacher told her class each and every school day morning.

As he played in the school playground each morning and afternoon with his friends, the older children would tell them to stay away from the wizened old crow, or she would boil them in oil and then eat them for her supper. She will call out to you by your name but do not go near her, for if you do, you will not return, the older children had said.

Every Sunday the minister from his pulpit at church spoke against her with venom. She is the living devil amongst us, beware of her evil and vile ways, he preached at the men, women and children of his small parish. She worships the devil in every possible conceivable disgusting manner, for she is one of the most willing, damnable, demonic disciples, he preached to his entire flock. All the population of the village attended church - the weak, the old, the young and the dying. She alone never went, nor would she be invited, ever.

No matter how hard he tried to recall how he had first met her, it always evaded his searching, enquiring mind. For that first and fateful encounter was the reason for his current unending predicament. There had to be a reason why he had gone to see her that first time. He could remember that he had been curious and puzzled by the constant never-ending flow of warnings given about her. Not just to him but to everyone that lived in or passed through the small village. Yet it constantly eluded him each time he sought the answer, the reason why he would have gone to see her, this evil woman. There had to be an answer somewhere in his mind, the answer he longed for. But it lay undisturbed no matter how hard he tried to remember.

He was certain that it was not because of the secret. For he did not, at that time, know that she was the protector of the secret. No one in the village, the schoolmistress in class, the minister from his pulpit or his parents at home - had ever made mention of a secret. She herself had told him about the dark secret - that much he knew, but wished he did not. It was not on his first, second or even third visit to her dark damp and secluded cottage that she had first made mention of it. But then it was all so, so very long ago.

Even his first recollections of her were hazy and blurred, except that he remembered his surprise that she was neither wizened nor old. His first memory of her, although sketchy now, had her dressed in black from her neck to her knees, her legs bare and her feet unshod - she had painted toenails. Only one candle lit the dark interior of the small room and the two little windows that faced the meadow were blackened by thick encrusted candle smoke - so you could neither see out of them, nor in. She must have been expecting him, for she had prepared for him a fizzy drink, which tickled and teased his taste buds as he drank it. Then he remembered walking home and being scolded by his mother for being out so late.

He was old enough to be aware that, by going to see her, he would be severely punished by his parents and ostracised by the remainder of the village folk. They had never found out that, against all their dire warnings, he was visiting her, with an unstoppable regularity - until it was too late, and by then he was beyond caring what they thought. She had started reading to him soon after his thirteenth birthday, from a book that she always had on top of the table, next to the candle. It was a larger book than any of the books he had seen at school. It was bound in black leather that was old and smelled musty. To begin with, and for quite some considerable time, he had never really understood the meaning of any of the words that she read to him - he did not think to ask her why. But as he listened intently he felt relaxed and content. It was much, much later, almost two years, before he began to realise the true meaning of the words that she had been reading to him. It was then for the first time, on the eve of his fifteenth birthday, that she openly told him she was the guardian of the secret.

He could think of nothing else, it caressed him, it teased him, it gave him such pleasure, such joy, when he thought of it - for he could do little else then. His parents thought he was ill, the village doctor said it was a fever that would pass - yet it never did. She taught him to control his feelings, his emotions, and hide within himself, so that his mother and father believed the fever had passed. Nothing could be further from the truth, it burned strongly within him, tantalising his every waking moment, in all his thoughts and deeds. He knew then that, more than anything else, he wanted to be the next keeper of the secret.

You are the one to whom I shall pass the secret - that is the sole reason I have been reading you the knowledge from the book. You will be the next custodian, you need not fear, the secret will by yours when the time is right, when you are fully prepared. She had told him this when he had asked when it would be his. A promise one day, a retraction the next - the time must be right, you are not yet ready - she would say. He tried to force her to keep her promise, by staying away from her for days on end, but the unseen hold she had over him always forced him to go back to her. He would beg her forgiveness in fear that she would go back on her word. Have patience my young one, you must exercise restraint, for, come the day, it will be yours.

Then came the day he knew would come eventually, when he was seen by some village folk as he left her dark cottage. He felt no fear as he crossed the meadow towards his parent's house, it was as if he were at a crossroads, deciding which road to take. They would not let him enter the house, the doors were locked, the windows shut. You are evil, a follower of the she-devil, you cannot live here ever again, go back to your witch where you now belong, his parents had shouted at him before the crowd had assembled. Enraged at his perceived treacherousness against them, they directed obscenities at him and then began throwing stones at him, forcing him away from the village, across the meadow towards the edge of the forest. What did he care what they thought, soon he would have the secret.

She had opened the door and stepped outside as the mob approached her cottage forcing him before them. When they saw her they turned and ran as fast as they could back towards the village. She tended to his cuts and bruises caused by the stones and the pain he had felt quickly vanished. He saw a bed already prepared for him over by the blackened windows - she knew he would not be going back to his home or the village, ever. Like her he was now to be feared, detested and shunned from that day forever more.

Soon after he had moved into the dark cottage, small noticeable changes began within him. His hunger began to diminish, and he ate less and less as each day passed. His thirst dried up and soon he hardly touched a drop of water or any other liquid. Yet his young supply body remained strong and healthy, even though his needs diminished more and more - until they completely stopped. He had questioned her about it, hoping that now he was truly to become the keeper - maybe this was what she was waiting for, he thought. Soon, she had replied, it will not be long now, she had said.

He knew that he was completely in her power, everything she bid him do, he did. She played with him, she teased him, she tormented at will, she took him to her bed. At first it was exciting, a new undiscovered pleasure, discovered. She had been gentle at first and he had enjoyed their mutual sexual pleasures. But as time passed her demeanour changed, as she began to demand more of him, and she was cruel if he showed resistance. She was now never satisfied with his sexual endeavours, she would tell him. She demanded more, always more. Days would pass when she would not let him out of her bed. Even on the few occasions when he had tried to leave her side - she would whisper to him, remember the secret, and he would turn back to her taking her in his powerful arms once more.

She had by this time stopped reading to him from the old black leather bound book. Why? he had asked. There is no longer any need she had replied simply. It was then that a sudden chill overwhelmed him when he realised that for him there was a need, for it was the book that was the keeper, the book was the true guardian of the secret. Once you had read the whole book you only became part of the secret. She had used the book to ensnare him in her web of deceit and lies, and she had completed her task well. He had been a fool to have believed that she would ever let him know how to get closer to the secret - for she would have lost her precious hold over him.

She still wandered amongst the trees and the paths of the forest, occasionally crossing the meadow towards the village. So, without her permission, he took every opportunity to read the book in her absence. For, in order to control him, she had read him enough of the book for him to now understand the meaning of the strange words. He took great care that she did not discover what he was doing when she was away from her cottage, and slowly but surely he began to uncover the secret contained in the musty-smelling old book. As the months came and went, as the seasons changed one following another - his mind grew stronger as time slowly moved along.

He watched her very closely as he began to take control. Little by little he was becoming stronger mentally, while she began to weaken. He was still careful not to defy her outright, yet in most things he had his way. As he approached the ending of the book, he could feel the power growing inside him. That which he had yearned and longed for so much was about to become his. She began to grow old before his eyes as the days and nights passed. Her wandering days were now over, she had become far too weak to leave her bed, let alone the cottage. Her sexual appetite had deserted her - he felt no pity, why should he? It was she who had ensnared him and kept him a virtual prisoner in her cottage for the past fifteen years. Even as a boy he had been her slave.

As he watched her become wizened and aged, all of his thoughts were concentrated on finishing the reading of the book. And on the day when he at last accomplished his task and learned the true secret of the book, he rushed to her room, which he had not entered for weeks, only to find a pile of grey ash on the bed where she had lain.

He screamed aloud, but no one heard. The very secret he had sought had killed her, as it was bound to do - for it was written that whosoever completes the reading of the book will enjoy life eternal until another comes and completes the task. Then the guardian of the book will perish to allow the other to take their place.

The minister from his pulpit each and every Sunday tells his flock to stay away from the warlock, the evildoer that wanders in the forest and in the fields. The school teacher tells his pupils not to go near the old dark cottage by the edge of the forest. The parents tell their children to stay away from the man dressed in black, for he is a servant of the devil.

Waiting

Martha looked at the large ornate imitation marble clock sitting on top of the mantelpiece, a wedding present from a distant relative to her mum all those years ago. Three hours had elapsed since he'd received the phone call, got his work things together and put on his grubby raincoat because the forecast had said heavy rain later. He hadn't said anything and she hadn't asked, it had been that way now for several years. A silent acknowledgement by the both of them, she must never inquire about his business and he'd never mention it either. Deep down of course she wanted to know, I mean who wouldn't, it was the uncertainty, not knowing and to an extent not caring, but only when she was down, feeling there had to be something better in her life than mere acquiescence. In part it was her fault, she should have said something at the beginning, yet she'd chosen not to, not because she was frightened of him, he'd never hurt her, either physically or mentally, well not intentionally anyway.

When mum passed away he'd been a source of comfort back then, a shoulder to cry on, a tower of strength helping her cope with her grief. They'd been close, she and her mum, some might say too close but she never regretted staying at home all those years while the few friends she knew got engaged, married, then kids. Her dad had died in an accident, hit by a drunk driver when she was five, her reminiscences of him were vague and sketchy. Mum got rid of the photos, made her cry every time she saw him. They moved home shortly afterwards, mum saying later they had to, without dad's wages they needed a smaller house.

She hears the rain battering on the windows, its heavy like the forecast said earlier, so he was right to put on his raincoat before he left for his work. Maybe she should watch the television, take her mind off having to wait, wondering what he's up to and how long he might be. Saturday evening, Strictly and X Factor neither of them her cup of tea, although Bruce Forsythe could be a laugh when he messed things up. She picks up her knitting instead and adjusts the standard lamp behind her chair to get a better light. She's asked him on a number of occasions if they could get a brighter bulb but for some reason he keeps forgetting. She's knitting bootees for their neighbour Carol, who's due in five weeks, told her it's a boy so she chose blue. They can't have kids, she left it too late looking after mum all those years, he doesn't mind although she should have told him before they got married.

She startles slightly as the clock strikes eight, she'd been concentrating on her knitting, knit one purl one, basic really but she's not a great knitter. Mum had been, she'd sit by the fire with her wool basket and needles and make all kinds of stuff. She should have left, mum wasn't that ill really until just before she died. I don't blame her, I blame myself, she thought, she never asked me to stay but then again she never told me to go. She never met him, it was shortly after the funeral when she'd summoned up the courage to go to a pub. She'd tinkered with the idea of Internet dating but you read so many nasty stories in the press. He was kind, attentive, although a little shy, just like her. He works in an office, dull and boring he said and has an occasional part time job. He never told her what it was, she can't even remember why not, she thinks maybe sometime he said something about consultant work. They were married within weeks.

She glances at the clock and decides to have a drink so pours herself a largish sherry, it'll help her sleep later on. He left just before four so he's been out five hours now doing, well doing whatever it is he does. She knows she shouldn't worry, but she can't help herself, things keep popping into her mind. His bag, he never lets her see what's inside it, she knows it's heavy by the way he carries it. He never lets her clean his clothes, says he prefers to do it himself, always has done. Even his leather shoes he cleans meticulously especially the soles, which she considers strange although she's never questioned him about it. He's a loner, has no friends, same as her really, although she does have one or two work acquaintances who invite her out for the odd spot of lunch.

She finishes her sherry and washes the glass. She stands by the sink watching the water drain away. Normally she'd go to bed, try and read and end up worrying as usual. But not tonight, tonight she was going to ask him what he gets up to when he gets these phone calls, gets his bag and leaves her there worrying herself to death. She'd gone through his pockets; what wife wouldn't in the circumstances. Maybe he's cheating on me she thinks, the phone calls are always on his mobile, never the land line, are they from a woman she wonders? No, she'd know if that was the reason, he's not the type that would cheat on his wife. She hears a car door slam in the driveway, he's home.

He stands in the doorway dripping wet, surprised to see her still up and waiting for him. 'I'll make you a nice cup of tea dear,' she says, her voice trembling slightly. She knows he always goes to the kitchen when he gets back.

'No thanks love, I need to clean up, why don't you go to bed, I'll be there shortly,' his tone of voice is authoritative.

'Well let me take your coat off and put your bag away, it's the least I can do,' she sees the look in his eyes, he's confused, not entirely sure how to react.

'What's this about, Martha?' It's a simple question.

She blurts it all out, holding nothing back, the questions coming easily and quickly one after another, followed by tears which cascade down her face. He drops the bag, it makes a resounding crash as it hits the floor. Through wet eyes she sees him walk towards her and feels his strong arms around her. 'Hush, hush love, there's no need to cry, I'll explain everything, have a seat in the lounge, I'll be there in a minute.'

She hears him in the kitchen; the water's running as usual, then the pantry door where he keeps his shoe cleaning kit. She sits wringing her hands between her knees wondering if she's done the right thing, he wasn't angry, he was calm.

He sits opposite her and eases his bag onto the carpet then pushes it towards her slowly with his foot. 'Have a look inside Martha, it should explain a lot,' he says calmly.

Her fingers are shaking as she fumbles with the clip then the zip. She hesitates before undoing it and looks up into his eyes. He nods, giving approval for what she is about to do. There were tools, not workman's tools, these were specialist implements a surgeon would use and she should know, she'd seen them often enough in the course of her work as a nurse. There were bone cutters, several lancets, two saws of different sizes for sawing through bone, a small spade, two packs of anti-septic cleaning wipes and some black plastic bin liners.

'I'm called upon occasionally. I'm a specialist Martha, a cleaner of sorts; I dispose of other peoples cock-ups.'

She looks at him through eyes full of tears sitting there calm, self-assured as if he didn't have a care in the world, her mind is racing but she doesn't know what to think.

'I don't kill anyone Martha, they're already dead,' he says simply as she holds back tears trying to make sense of it all.

'Problem is Martha, it's because I'm good at what I do. I'm the expert everyone wants. I can't get out, they won't let me. It's been like this for years, I'm stuck in a rut.'

Weekend Break

It was raining hard, literally throwing it down as Gordon steered the car cautiously between the two grey concrete posts with the windscreen wipers going full bore. 'We've made it,' he sighed with relief. The journey had taken much longer than expected due to the inclement weather and surprisingly the weight of traffic he'd not expected.

'Over there Gordon, I can see an empty space just by the two large dustbins,' Mildred said as she peered through the gloom and the rain. 'Look just next to that old Land Rover, the one with the bike attached to the back.'

'Got it,' Gordon put the car in gear and inched the car forwards occasionally giving the misted up windscreen a wipe with an old worn shammy to try and help him improve his vision. It hadn't helped that he'd forgotten to re-gas the air-conditioning in the car before they'd left.

'You know we're going to get soaked by the time we reach the front door,' she remarked frostily just as he'd finished reversing.

Gordon let out another sigh, much much deeper now. 'Do you want me to drive around to the front?' His tone was acquiescent, her remark was not out of character.

'No, we're here now and I have an umbrella, you'll just have to make two trips. You know I can't carry anything heavy what with my bad back.'

'Doesn't stop you going dancing and to that expensive pilates class,' Gordon said softly under his breath as he turned and peered into the rear of the car. 'Where's my raincoat Mildred? I told you to put it in the back just before we left.

'Now just you look here Gordon, my doctor said gentle exercise was good for me and for your information I pay for my pilates out of my bingo winnings. So just stop with your moaning for goodness sake we're on holiday. Oh! and I never heard you say a word about your raincoat, so if it's not here you must have left it. Now get the cases, I'm off to reception to see about our room.' Mildred opened the car door, raised her umbrella, then headed off towards the entrance.

Gordon watched her go and wondered why on earth he'd ever agreed to go on a weekend break with a wife he despised with a vengeance. As a rule they simply accepted each other's company when at home as they just sat there watching television all evening with barely a word exchanged between them before it was off to separate bedrooms. Mildred's poor back was the excuse she had made when he'd returned home one afternoon to find she'd put all his nightwear in the spare room. 'We'll try it for a week or so until my back gets better,' she'd said and that was close on two years now. He'd tried to sneak in one night when he was feeling frisky and she'd sent him packing with, 'Gordon no! I have my poor back to think of. Why don't you take a cold shower.'

Then he remembered the reason he'd agreed to the weekend away, of course a hotel, one double room, so just maybe she would forget all about her damned back, she had been a good lover once.

'Come on Gordon, get a move on I've made the arrangements a double room with separate beds.' Mildred turned her attention back to the young male receptionist. 'It is a room with a sea view?' she enquired with a smile.

'Yes Mrs Williams, just as you requested,' he replied as he passed over the room key, 'number 207 on the second floor. Breakfast is from seven-thirty to ten and dinner is at seven. I hope you both enjoy your stay and if there's anything at all I can do for you then don't hesitate to ask.'

'Thank you,' Mildred looked at his name badge displayed on his uniform then flashed her eyes in his direction, 'Steven, I'm sure we will.'

Gordon noticed she was giving the receptionist one of her special smiles, the one that said, *'I'm yours if you play your cards right.'* He was sure she never went to bingo every time she said she was going, but he'd not been able to follow her as she always took the car. Then there were her so-called winnings every time she played, well he wasn't a complete fool, but then again he'd never confronted her about it.

'Move yourself Gordon the lift is over there, here take the key, I'll be up I a moment.' There was no mistaking the authority in her voice.

Soaking wet he set off for the lift with a suitcase in each hand. As he waited for it to arrive he could hear the sound of laughter coming from the reception desk, Mildred had already made a friend and they'd been there less than five minutes. The room was small yet cosy and the beds were separated by a bedside cabinet with a telephone on the top. He dropped the cases and walked into the small en-suite where he picked up a towel to dry his head and face. Maybe Mildred had decided her back was no longer a problem and this was to be a romantic weekend, although the single beds were a downer unless she thought them more exciting. He took the decision there and then looking into the small mirror that no matter what, he was going to do his best to be courteous, kind and, if allowed, even affectionate.

'Gordon let me in,' Mildred shouted from the corridor, 'you could have left the door open.'

They unpacked in silence and when Gordon had finished putting his clothes away in the small drawers provided he turned the television on then sat on the bed nearest the door. 'Is it okay if I have this one?'

'Of course, you know I like to be next to the window,' she replied before walking into the en-suite to deal with the toiletries, 'and turn the television off I feel I have a headache coming on.'

Gordon suggested a walk along the front before dinner, she refused although it had stopped raining. A drink in the bar was another suggestion he advanced, but no, she'd have a glass of wine with her meal. So for two hours they sat on their respective beds, he reading from his Kindle while Mildred dealt with her nails on her hands and feet. She was still an attractive woman at the age of fifty-six and always took care of her appearance. They sat by themselves which had surprised him as there were other guests in the dining room with spare places at their tables. His spirits rose when she actually proposed a toast with her wine. 'Here's to a nice break,' she said.

'I'll drink to that Mildred, maybe we can have a walk along the prom before we turn in?' he suggested as a vision of them walking hand-in-hand along the prom materialised in his mind. It was the kind of thing they had done on a regular basis before they were married.

'Don't be stupid Gordon it's still raining out there,' replied Mildred before popping a piece of Chicken Kiev into her mouth.

Disappointed yet undeterred Gordon picked up the bottle of house white and poured a large measure into Mildred's empty glass. Maybe if he managed to get her tipsy she might be more agreeable to sharing her bed with him later on.

'Gordon you know I don't ever drink more than the one glass, you'll just have to finish that off yourself or keep it for dinner tomorrow,' said Mildred, the moment she noticed how full her glass was.

Damn and blast it, would she never allow herself to relax. 'Sorry my dear, I just thought you know that, being on a weekend break, you might let your hair down as it were,' he said softly before picking up her glass and taking a hefty slug from it.

'Well if you're going to drink it all then make sure you brush your teeth before going to your bed and make sure you keep your face turned away from my bed,' said Mildred haughtily as she added more salt to her meal.

In an instant with that remark she had dashed all of his hopes that he might have been lucky enough to have sex with his wife that night. Every fibre in his body was screaming at him to toss the wine in her face and call her a frigid cow but somehow he managed to resist the strong temptation. Luckily the wine glass he was clasping so firmly didn't break and he replaced it gently down on the table hoping she hadn't noticed his shaking hand. It was at that precise moment that Gordon took the decision to murder his wife and it wasn't because she had refused him sex for the past two years, there were a multitude of different reasons now he came to think about it. Belittling him constantly in public every time they went shopping, telling their few friends he was a useless individual when it came to doing any house improvements. Refusing to allow members of his family to come for a visit. Then there was the occasion when he'd taken a stray dog from the pound and she'd made him take it back. The only question to which he now needed an answer was how was he going to do it?

'Gordon concentrate on eating your food, I've finished mine and I want to order my sweet,' said Mildred loudly so the other guests could hear.

Her words broke his chain of thought. 'What? Food, right, yes of course dear, sorry I was day dreaming.'

'Yes well that's just typical of you isn't it, useless that's what you are,' she said, pleased that she now had an audience listening in. 'Honestly Gordon, I sometimes wonder why I ever married you, you can be so tiresome you know.'

This was a typical ploy of hers to start an argument so she could put him in his place. Well he wasn't going to fall for it this time. He leaned across the table and said quietly. 'Not tonight Mildred, please, no arguments this evening.'

'Huh, wimp,' she caught sight of the waiter and raised a hand.

'Yes madam?'

'May I have the dessert menu?'

'Certainly madam, coffee or a liqueur and perhaps sir would prefer a brandy?' he let the questions hang.

'Sir will have black coffee only, he's already had far too much alcohol to drink. I shall have a cafe latte thank you.'

'Certainly madam, I'll fetch the sweet trolley,' said the waiter before heading into the kitchen with the order for the drinks.

'*Poison*,' thought Gordon then instantly discarded it, too uncertain and he didn't know where he could get his hands on any. *'Suicide, yes that might work,'* he beamed a broad smile at Mildred.

'What on earth are you grinning at? You look like a cat who's got hold of the cream.' Mildred was perplexed, her husband didn't usually grin at her.

'Oh sorry my dear, I was just thinking about something, nothing to concern yourself about my dear.'

'Well don't do it again, it's rather unnerving you know.'

'God I wish I had done it before.' Yes, suicide would be perfect but by what method.

'More water sir,' enquired a passing waiter.

'No I'm fine thank you.' Water yes, drowning might work, she couldn't swim but it would be difficult to get her on a beach or to a deserted swimming pool, so it would have to be something else. There was of course the marina where small boats and a few larger yachts were moored, that would be an ideal location and it was secluded. He'd noticed it through the rain when they had driven into the town. 'Mildred, you were correct my dear, I have drunk too much wine so I'll have a bit of a walk, perhaps you'd care to join me?' he enquired knowing what her response would be. He was going to have a good look around and pick out the best place where with luck he could push her in.

Mildred was just about to object when she noticed the young man Steven, the receptionist, walk into the dining room and speak to a waiter. 'Well if you feel you must then you do that Gordon but I won't be accompanying you and don't blame me when you catch a chill.' Although she had been speaking directly to her husband her hazel brown eyes were fixed on Steven.

She doesn't even care that I know she's got the hots for the receptionist he thought just as the waiter arrived with the sweet trolley. As usual she chose the chocolate gateau with lashings of double cream for herself and two small piece of cheese for Gordon. 'You have to be careful with your weight, you've gained quite a few pounds in the last few months,' she said knowing it to be an untruth.

'*Just you wait you bitch, you'll be sorry then,*' he thought as he picked up a piece of limp cheddar with a knife. 'My doctor wouldn't agree with you there Mildred, he weighed me less than two weeks ago and told me I'd lost half a stone.' He hadn't told her about the pains in his stomach or his visits to see Dr Barnsley over the past nine months. She would have told him he was being a wimp, real men don't see doctors had been a favourite expression of hers when he'd gone down with glandular fever two years into their marriage.

Another wedge of gateaux disappeared before Mildred spoke. 'Oh, so you've seen the doctor have you, well please enlighten me Gordon, what was it this time, a slight headache perhaps?' she enquired caustically.

Gordon ignored the question, she was clearly up for another public argument. He finished his coffee then stood up. 'I'm going to reception to see if I can borrow an umbrella and ask for a spare key. I wouldn't want to disturb you when I get back.'

'Take your time Gordon, if that's what you want to do then do it.' She was pleased he was going out as it would give her the opportunity to flirt with Steven, maybe he could get away from reception for a short while.

It was just over a mile from the hotel to the marina and the rain had eased off by the time he arrived there. Luckily the tide was in as the boats were riding high in the water which was a relief to Gordon who'd been considering what he might do if the tide had been out. They were only here for the three nights and the tide did not change that dramatically but now as he looked down into the dark black water a slow smile crossed his face. It had just gone nine and the place appeared completely deserted. Ten minutes later after he'd completed a full circumnavigation of the marina he knew this was the perfect spot to kill his wife. It was poorly lit with only six of the eleven lampposts actually working, even the solitary telephone booth was out of action with no illumination. None of the boats were lit including the larger ones and he'd come across a notice stating a large fine would be imposed if any owner was found to be living onboard. The only problem he could foresee was how he was going to persuade Mildred to come with him on a walk to the marina?

'Did you enjoy your walk sir?' enquired Steven with a smirk he tried to hide when Gordon returned the umbrella two hours later.

'Yes I did, thank you,' there was no point in being rude or upset with the young man, it was hardly his fault his wife had the hots for him. He'd gone to a pub after the marina to have a drink and reflect on how he was going to get Mildred down to the marina when it was dark. Although he hadn't been there during the day, it would be far too risky to dispose of her in broad daylight and someone might even jump in to save her, he couldn't allow that, no way.

Steven just couldn't resist gloating. 'Mrs Williams seemed in good spirits the last time I saw her,' he said just as her husband was about to walk away. In fact the last time he'd seen her was half an hour ago when they made love in the linen closet. She had been quite forceful with him which had been a first for him.

Gordon didn't turn around, what was the point. Carefully he inserted his key into the lock and entered the room as quietly as possible. By the time he went to bed he knew she wasn't asleep, she was only pretending as her breathing was irregular and erratic. She was no doubt recalling her amorous adventure in the linen cupboard. Once in bed he turned his face away as instructed and before long he was fast asleep happy in the knowledge he was going to do away with her sometime during the weekend.

Surprisingly the following day turned out to be rather nice on two counts, the weather improved to the extent that the sun stayed out all day and Mildred even appeared to actually enjoy herself. Her only complaint was that she now wished she had booked the hotel for a week instead of the three days. 'It's such a lovely spot isn't it Gordon,' she'd remarked over lunch in a pub by the seafront.

It's only lovely because of the young athletic receptionist Steven back at the hotel thought Gordon but refrained from saying so. 'Yes it's a nice place. I'm sure we could extend our stay if you really wanted to,' he suggested as it would give him longer to complete his planning.

'Well yes, but then I do have my pilates class on Wednesday and I can't afford to miss that, pity though I really do like it here.'

The pilates instructor was a man in his early thirties who Gordon had looked up on the internet when Mildred had first started attending on a regular basis. She never even attempted to explain why the sessions took nearly three hours but then again how could she when the extra hour and a half was spent somewhere else with him. That was about the time he'd been dispatched to the spare room now he came to think about it. 'Why don't you book one extra night then and we'll travel back on Tuesday instead,' he proffered lightly hoping she'd take it up, one extra day was better than nothing and it would give him more thinking time of how to get her to the marina.

Her eyes gleamed at the thought. 'Yes Gordon, I'll do that,' she answered almost instantly, hoping of course Steven would be on duty, she'd forgotten to ask him yesterday. If he wasn't then she'd make some excuse for not staying another night with her husband in the room. She was at a complete loss as to why she had suggested this trip with Gordon tagging along in the first place.

The remainder of the day turned out to be uneventful as they did what tourists to the seaside usually did by visiting the waxworks, followed by the amusement arcade where Gordon might have expected her to play her favourite game, bingo, but she was not interested. When they arrived back at the hotel Mildred told Gordon she was going to have a rest and made it plain she wanted to be alone. Gordon hardly shrugged his shoulders and walked into the bar, he'd completely given up on having any kind of sexual relations with his wife. He was however interested to see what happened when she approached the reception so he chose a chair with a view into the reception area. By the antics displayed by Mildred it was clear she had found out that the young receptionist would still be on duty for the next three nights.

By Monday night Gordon had still not managed to persuade Mildred to accompany him on his evening walk, he was now getting desperate as there was only more more night left before they would set off for home. Having returned from the marina he went into the bar and ordered a large whisky before sitting down, he still had some thinking to do. Then before his drink arrived he suddenly came up with an idea, but would she buy it, that was the big question?

'Gordon have you gone completely insane? How can you possibly be thinking of such a thing?' Mildred asked incredulously as she looked at her husband across the dining table.

'I'm not thinking about it my dear, I'm going to sign the papers before we head for home tomorrow morning,' he lied. Now he had to convince her that what he was about to do was genuine.

'But that money is our savings Gordon, you can't possibly be thinking of purchasing a boat. You've gone crazy, tell me this is a joke,' there was a pleading look in Mildred's eyes, this couldn't be happening. Had he found out about her affairs? Was this his way of getting back at her by teasing her.

How lucky he was to have insisted on keeping their savings in his name at the building society. It was nearly all his money anyway as Mildred had stopped working two months after they were married. He'd thought she was preparing to have children but she soon informed him otherwise. 'Kids running about the house making a mess, me dealing with filthy nappies, you must be joking,' she'd said and now here she was thinking he was joking again. 'It's no joke Mildred but if you hadn't insisted on this weekend away then maybe I'd never have thought of it, but seeing all those lovely boats in the marina I just couldn't resist. Just imagine what lovely holidays we can have sailing across to France and even further.' He was really enjoying himself watching her sitting in front of him with her mouth and eyes wide open in utter amazement at what he was saying.

Mildred exploded. 'What! Are you telling me that's it's my fault you've gone and done something stupid like buying a stupid silly boat just because I wanted to come to the seaside?'

Gordon allowed a smile to cross his face before he answered, 'Well it's a fact Mildred, had we not been here I wouldn't have been out walking on my own every night. Anyway, as I said, I'm going ahead with it tomorrow but why don't you come to the marina and see for yourself you might fall in love with it as I did.'

Mildred suddenly saw a possible way out of this nightmare that had just been sprung on her. She would accept the offer and then point out everything that was wrong with the stupid boat even if there wasn't. She had to do something to stop him from going ahead with the purchase. 'Of course I want to see whatever it is you're going to waste our hard earned savings on, we'll go immediately after dinner is finished.'

'But it will be dark my dear wouldn't you prefer to see it first thing in the morning when it's light?' He knew he wasn't taking a risk as there was no way she was going to delay.

'That won't matter. Ahem, how much have you said you will pay for it?'

He leaned slightly across the table then answered, 'It's a real bargain, only forty-eight thousand two hundred and some small change.'

Mildred's eyebrows shot up in abject horror, 'Christ Gordon that's very nearly all of my money.' As soon as the words were out of her mouth Mildred knew she'd made a grave error.

Gordon sat back in his chair then said quietly but in a steely tone, 'My money, Mildred! Is that what you just said?' He held a hand aloft. 'No don't bother replying, I have good hearing and you know very well that apart from a few pounds all of that money came from my wages, not yours. Now let's stop arguing and enjoy our dinner.'

He knows about Steven that's for sure or he wouldn't be sitting there with such bravado, this wasn't the man she was married to. Something had changed in him, he was now confident, self-assured, sitting opposite her as if he didn't have a care in the world. She had to do something to alter his perspective. 'Gordon, maybe we could have a little bit of fun before we go and have a look at this boat. It would be rather nice squeezed together in the small bed,' she flashed her eyes in a provocative manner.

She's actually trying to bribe me with sex, the silly woman, which goes to show how desperate she is to distract me, he thought. Looking her straight in her come-hither eyes he said, 'If the offer is still available after we've been to the marina I don't see why not, it's been quite a while Mildred since you and I last made love.'

She wasn't sure how to respond, knowing it was because of her actions by banishing him to the spare room two years ago, 'Well yes, but it would be nice to make up for lost time.' She had to try and keep him sweet no matter the cost. She'd been planning to start divorce proceedings soon and had already talked to a lawyer who'd told her she was entitled to half of everything. 'Come on Gordon, let's have a bit of fun and you never know, I might actually like,' she paused not wanting to say the next words, 'the boat you're thinking of buying. She fluttered her eyelashes once more and thrust her boobs forwards.

Gordon was actually tempted for a few seconds before reality reasserted itself. 'I'd rather not Mildred, let's see how we feel after we've been to the marina.'

There was a quarter moon in the night sky as they approached the marina which disappeared now and then between heavy clouds threatening yet more rain. They hadn't exchanged a single word on the walk from the hotel but as they passed through the small wooden barriers at the entrance to the marina Mildred spoke, 'It's pretty dim in here, surely you didn't agree to buy a boat when you could hardly see it?'

'I saw all I wanted to see Mildred,' he replied simply as he recalled the previous evenings' walks around the marina when Mildred was entertaining Steven in the linen closet behind the reception desk.

'So where's this silly boat then?' Mildred cast her eyes around the line of gently bobbing boats in the still dark water of the marina.

'It's the first one just around this corner.' Gordon wanted to be completely out of sight of the entrance just in case somebody might pass by.

Mildred quickened her step, anxious to see the offending object. 'What on earth! Surely this is a joke you fool?'

The first boat was actually the small dredger they used to clear the silt from the marina bottom and looked like an old disused tug with an open filthy hold. Gordon actually smiled as he looked at the rusting vessel then, before Mildred could react, he grabbed her by the arm and hauled her to the quayside and shoved her as hard as he could. On the way down in her desperation she somehow managed to grab hold of his jacket and they both fell into the cold dark water. She was still clasping him, now with both hands, when they surfaced and she began to scream loudly.

'Oh damn,' said Gordon as he pulled her under the water just as a dark cloud covered the moon. It seemed rather ironic to Gordon, here she was fighting and clawing away at him for all she was worth, desperately trying to survive while he was already under a death sentence with his cancer, six months the doctors had said. What was a few months to him anyway and this way there would be no pain, no suffering. This hadn't been in his plan but now he was actually pleased they were both going to go together. He reasoned the authorities would put the drownings down to a tragic accident nothing more. The only person who might have doubts would be his doctor who was aware of his circumstances but he was hardly likely to suggest foul play. But then again what would it matter if he did. Gordon opened his mouth and took in as much water as he possibly could and held on tight to his wife as they began to sink slowly and silently to the bottom of the marina.

Number 47

'Liz don't you think there is something strange about number 47 across the road?' I enquire just as I am about to close our new window blinds.' We've been living in our little bungalow for several months now having returned from living abroad for twenty-two years.

My wife raises her head away from her smartphone and gives me a puzzled look. 'What do you mean, strange?' she asks giving me one of her quizzical looks that shows off her dazzling eyes to great effect.

'They never appear to put any lights on no matter how dark it gets and I've never seen either of them open the front door,' I proffer as I continue to look at the house with the Fiat Panda parked in the drive.

'I hadn't really noticed to be honest but it is odd the way he changes the cars around every morning.' Liz always makes the breakfast and from the kitchen window she has a direct view of number 47 across the street.

'Yes strange isn't it, he drives her car onto the road, opens their garage then drives his car into the street, parks it and then puts her car into the garage,' I agree just as I notice him come out of their side gate with a watering can. 'Look he's watering his garden again and it only rained last night.'

Liz approaches the window and looks out being careful not to move the still open blinds. 'Wonder how he got that large red mark on his forehead - probably a birthmark, or maybe an accident of some sort. What do you think?'

The man in question is middle aged around five eight or nine tall, slim build with dark hair turning grey and it's hard to miss the facial stain which was the colour of red wine. I have to say that we are not nosey people but our bungalow is very nearly directly opposite and when we have breakfast on our lap-trays we tend amongst other topics to discuss what is happening in the street. There is a green with half a dozen aged trees across from us and many of the neighbours and local children often congregate there to chat or play, so there is usually plenty going on to chat about. Now the lady at number 47 seems to be quite a recluse, we don't think she has a job as the car stays on the drive all day until her husband repeats the morning procedure the opposite way around when he arrives home in the afternoon. She wears black, always black, and seldom ventures out unless it is for the weekly shopping when they go in his car together. Shorter than him, probably around five five and thin, verging on anorexic going by how slim she appears in her black clothes, difficult to tell as we've never seen her in any other colour.

'It's quite large for a birthmark - I reckon it's more likely that it's a burn mark of some sort, perhaps he was in some sort of fire. Hey, he's finished and rushing back via the garden gate again,' I say just as a small white van drives up and parks outside number 47.

A tradesman of some sort gets out of the unmarked van walks up to the front door and rings the bell, then stands back a little waiting. Nobody responds to his ring so he leans forward after a minute or so and tries again before peering in through the frosted glass of the porch door. Clearly frustrated he walks slowly back to the van turning back to look at the house just in case someone might answer his ring.

'They never answer the front door do they?' Liz returns to the sofa, picks up her smartphone and I close the blinds.

'Never, not in the time we've been here, not once. Even when they've had deliveries the boxes always go in via the garage or the garden gate. Hey, have you ever wondered what might be in those boxes, they get quite a few of them delivered,' I ask as I begin to speculate what might be in them myself. 'Witches and warlock gear I reckon, think just how often she cleans the bedroom widows, it's every second day. Candle smoke can leave quite a few smears on glass and she's always at it. Perhaps his forehead was an accident with candles. Thinking about it we do see flickering lights showing through their Venetian blinds but we've never ever seen any electric ones not in all the time we've been here and we're in the middle of winter now when it gets dark around four in the afternoon, that's definitely odd,' I conclude.

'They're not witches, don't be daft,' Liz counters. 'Odd perhaps, but witches never. Maybe she works from home and the boxes are to do with her business,' she suggests after giving the question some consideration.

'That's possible I concede but tell me why neither of us have ever seen a real electric light on over there, because I certainly haven't.'

'That's true, I've never seen one either but maybe they are trying to save money or something,' says Liz shrugging her shoulders as she tries to concentrate on finishing her WhatsApp to a friend in Spain.

'Well I think they are a very strange couple, never answering their door and nobody lives in the dark unless they're weirdos. I'm going to get to the bottom of what it is they do over there. I'm convinced that there is something odd happening at number 47.'

'Okay you do what you want but don't involve me,' Liz hits send on her smartphone then closes the case.

Over the next few days I start a list of the comings and goings at 47 and by the end of the week I am surprised at how many times they have gone out around eleven o'clock just when we are getting ready for bed. This was something I hadn't noticed before but, to be fair, I hadn't been keeping an eye on them then. Three nights out of seven they got into his car dressed in black, he was even wearing a black tie and carrying a large holdall and yes it was black also. I tell Liz that I am going to follow them one night and she tells me I am nuts. We have a bit of an argument about my going out but in the end she reluctantly agrees provided I am careful and don't let them see me. So on the following Saturday at ten forty-five I get into my car wearing warm clothes as the temperature is only 3 degrees above freezing. I slump down in the driver's seat in case the headlights of his car catch me watching them. Then dead on eleven they appear, walking from the side gate dressed in their usual clothes. The streets are well lit so I use my sidelights and keep about one hundred yards behind them wondering how far they are going to drive. I'm surprised when they turn into a small road that will take them to the mere only two miles at the most from home. I know the mere well as we usually walk around it two or three times a week depending on the weather. I slow down knowing the only place they can stop would be in or near the car park so I wait a couple of minutes before I follow them. I park in the secondary car park off to the right switching off my side lights as I drive in quietly and to my surprise I notice several cars, including theirs, already parked in the primary one. Out of the car I keep as close as I can to the treeline and walk through the second gate and down towards the mere. I've completely forgotten to take a torch with me but the night is clear with a three-quarter moon casting shadows on the ground. I hear the sound of some laughter over to my left and cautiously walk towards it keeping in the shadows as much as possible. I'm grateful to Liz for reminding me to wear something warm as my exhaled breath forms a mist before my eyes in the moonlight. The laughter, louder now, suddenly dies and I immediately stop dead in my tracks wondering if they have seen me. After several anxious moments the laughter is replaced by low chanting and I am now able to see the outline of a group of robed people in a small clearing. I circle slowly and cautiously round to my right until I come to a tall spruce tree I am able to hide behind. Peering round cautiously I count eight robed figures standing before a tree stump that has a small object sitting on it but I'm not able to see what it is from where I am positioned. The chanting grows a little louder just as one of the robed figures approaches the trunk and pours what looks like blood onto the object. I get my smartphone from my pocket and switch it on being careful to keep the light hidden in my hand. I start the camera app and take off the flash, that is the last thing I want. I adjust the zoom control to its maximum then I step forward to get a closer view and unfortunately step on a dead branch that gives what seems like an enormous crack. Immediately eight pair of eyes look towards the tree where I'm standing so I take off at speed and don't stop until I'm back at my car. No-one appears to be following but I start the car and drive home.

'You're having me on,' says Liz when I've finished regaling her with the night's events. 'You've been at the pub and had a drink or two,' she adds after a pause.

I get out my smartphone having heard it click a few times as I was running back to the car with it in my hand. 'Maybe this will prove that I was down by the mere,' I say as I scan the photos in the camera app. 'Have a look at these my love, they are dark but you can at least see where I've been,' I say with a beaming smile across my face.

Liz takes the phone and looks down at the photos zooming in on a couple of them. 'Look you can make out there are eight people here,' she holds it up for me to see.

'I know, I was there, and this proves it, now what do you have to say?' I ask confidently.

'Right, so they are a bit odd and have a get together in the woods, we're all different Martin.'

'But what about the blood?'

'You said you were too far away, it was probably red wine or Ribena maybe.'

'And the chanting?'

Look Martin I don't really care if eight consenting adults have a soiree in the wood late at night. You've proved your point, they are an odd couple. Now put it to bed because that's where I'm off to now, are you coming?'

Of course Liz was right, what business was it of mine if a bunch of kooks get together to chant around a tree stump in the dead of night, Maypole dancers do it in broad daylight. So I resolve to put it all behind me and get on with my own life. Which in truth I do until about three weeks later when I see a young man ring the front door bell, but getting no reply this time he walks around the side and enters the garden. I think this is interesting given the fact that the gate is open and, as time goes by, he doesn't re-appear either. He hadn't as far as I can tell arrived in a vehicle and by the time Liz gets back from her table tennis he is still inside. 'He must be a friend, people have them you know Martin,' she says after I explain the situation.

I drop the subject and go back to my writing. Then much later as I am switching off the television I notice the headlights of the car belonging to number 47 through our blinds so I carefully peek out. The boot is open and the two of them are lifting something heavy and awkward into it. Rushing into the hall I grab my winter coat and car keys putting my smartphone into my pocket. 'Liz I'm going out for a drive I won't be long,' I shout as I open the front door.'

'For goodness sake Martin, drop it,' she yells from the bedroom.

They are well gone by the time I get the car started but I know where they are going so I drive directly to the mere. I park in the same place and am surprised to see at least twelve cars in the main car park. The half moon does not provide as much illumination as the last time and I'm sure I'm making a lot more noise as I make my way towards the old spruce. If anything the chanting is louder than before probably because there are more of them at it. I raise the binoculars that we keep in the car and focus on the group. The candles around the stump give off an eerie glow and I am horrified to see the body of the young man I'd seen earlier in the day slumped over the stump bound hand and foot and he appears to be unconscious. Taking a few careful steps back but staying out of sight I call the police on my phone. 'There is a murder about to happen at the mere, approximately five hundred yards due east of the car park, get here quick,' I whisper before breaking the connection. I cautiously return to my hiding place desperately hoping the police will arrive soon.

'Sergeant I've just had a prank call, some nutter saying a murder is about to be committed down by the mere,' says police constable Mavis Jennings who is manning the emergency line that night.

'Why do you think he was a nutter Mavis?' enquires the sergeant slowly raising both eyebrows as he does so.

Mavis gives the question some thought then says, 'Well he was sort of whispering sergeant.'

'Could be Mavis that he didn't want other people to hear him. Was he on a land line or mobile?'

Mavis looks down at her console, 'Mobile sergeant.'

'Well send a car and then ring him back and tell him we're on our way.'

I had moved cautiously back to the spruce to watch the proceedings hoping the police would get here soon as I hadn't a clue what I could do alone to help the young man slumped over the tree stump. The chanting starts to get louder and louder until it suddenly stops and one robed figure steps forward and turns to face the rest of them throwing back his hood. It's the bloke from number 47, I'm sure of it, although I can't see his face clearly the red stain on his forehead is enough to identify him. Suddenly my phone starts to play the first four notes of Beethoven's fifth. Oh why didn't I mute it I think as I desperately try to switch it off. The chanting has stopped and the entire group are turned in my direction. By the time I manage to stop my phone ringing six robed figures are rushing towards me. I do the only thing possible, I turn to run but trip over a loose branch and hit my head on a tree. As I fall headlong into the scrub I can hear police sirens in the distance just before I slip into unconsciousness.

'We'll let you tell him all about it but let him know he'll have to make a statement when he's feeling better,' I hear the police sergeant say before he leaves the hospital room where I'm lying in bed with a bandage round my head.

Liz nods her head in agreement then turns towards me, 'Come on Martin, he's gone you can stop pretending to be still asleep.'

I open my eyes slowly letting them scan the room before I sit up in bed. 'Go on then tell me all about it, he said you could.'

Liz takes a deep breath then speaks, 'Well believe it or not you were right, he is a warlock and she is a witch. The coven apparently has been meeting by the mere for the past two years and they were intending that young man some harm. They have all been charged with assault and possession of a deadly weapon. The police aren't sure if they were actually going to murder him as they had plenty of chicken blood up there but they did drug him and the police are now doing other tests. They've searched the house and those boxes they had delivered had more robes, candles and a lot of other occult stuff. And I hate to admit this Martin but yes, they also had candles all over the place in every single room according to the sergeant. By the way, you have a slight concussion but they are discharging you in the morning. What have you to say to all of that?'

'Doesn't explain why they never opened their front door, does it?'